Clown Child

AMY LITTLESUGAR

illustrated by KIMBERLY BULCKEN ROOT

PHILOMEL BOOKS

For all my friends at Holly Center. —*A.L.*

To Janna, with love. —*K.B.R.*

Patricia Lee Gauch, Editor

PHILOMEL BOOKS
A division of Penguin Young Readers Group.
Published by The Penguin Group.
Penguin Group (USA) Inc., 375 Hudson Street, New York, NY 10014, U.S.A.
Penguin Group (Canada), 90 Eglinton Avenue East, Suite 700, Toronto, Ontario, Canada M4P 2Y3 (a division of Pearson Penguin Canada Inc.).
Penguin Books Ltd, 80 Strand, London WC2R 0RL, England.
Penguin Ireland, 25 St. Stephen's Green, Dublin 2, Ireland (a division of Penguin Books Ltd.).
Penguin Group (Australia), 250 Camberwell Road, Camberwell, Victoria 3124, Australia (a division of Pearson Australia Group Pty Ltd).
Penguin Books India Pvt Ltd, 11 Community Centre, Panchsheel Park, New Delhi - 110 017, India.
Penguin Group (NZ), Cnr Airborne and Rosedale Roads, Albany, Auckland 1310, New Zealand (a division of Pearson New Zealand Ltd).
Penguin Books (South Africa) (Pty) Ltd, 24 Sturdee Avenue, Rosebank, Johannesburg 2196, South Africa.
Penguin Books Ltd, Registered Offices: 80 Strand, London WC2R 0RL, England.

Text copyright © 2006 by Amy Littlesugar. Illustrations copyright © 2006 by Kimberly Bulcken Root.

Published simultaneously in Canada. Manufactured in China by South China Printing Co. Ltd.

Design by Semadar Megged. Illustrations were created with graphite pencil and watercolor on Arches 140 lb. hot-press paper.

Library of Congress Cataloging-in-Publication Data
Littlesugar, Amy. Clown child / Amy Littlesugar ; illustrated by Kimberly Bulcken Root. p. cm.
Summary: Olivia and her father are popular clowns in the Crystal Caravan circus, but she longs for a settled
home to live in. [1. Identity—Fiction. 2. Clowns—Fiction. 3. Circus—Fiction. 4. Fathers and daughters—Fiction. 5. Home—Fiction.] I. Root, Kimberly Bulcken, ill. II. Title. PZ7.L7362Clo 2006 [E]—dc22 2005019711

ISBN 0-399-23106-4
10 9 8 7 6 5 4 3 2 1
First Impression

In 1910, when cotton candy was called "fairy floss," a clown child named Olivia traveled with her father in a small mud circus known across the prairie as the Crystal Caravan.

Folks came from miles around to see the Famous Zorofsky, a trapeze artist with flying white hair. They came to see the brave Monsieur Jeanette, who had a way with the tigers. And they came to see the Tallest Man East of the Missouri.

But mostly they came just to laugh at Olivia's father, the Great Funnybones. The crowd would roar when his checkered pants caught fire, and cheer when Olivia, wearing a shiny red nose and big clown shoes, jumped in the ring to put the fire out.

"Ladies and gentlemen," the Great Funnybones would shout, "I give you the Amazing Pickles!"

At that moment, Olivia—her eyes closed—would step into the spotlight, stand on one foot, and juggle.

One, two, three, four. In a steady rhythm she'd send those eggs sailing into the air.

Drums rolled. Children squealed. The audience held its breath.

Then one, two, three, down came the eggs—SPLAT!

But everyone laughed and laughed and laughed.

"That's my girl," said the Great Funnybones with a wink.

But in the afternoon, when the performance ended and the Crystal Caravan was ready to move on to the next town, Olivia would say with real longing, "I'd sure like to have lived there, Pa."

More than anything in the world, Olivia wanted a real home. With curtains at the windows and wallpaper on the walls.

One evening, the Crystal Caravan pulled into Homersville, a small town at the fork of a big river. Olivia's job was to see to the animals. She unharnessed her pony, Bull's Eye, and let him graze beside the Indian elephants and Azarah, the little one-humped camel.

"Grub's on!" yelled the Tallest Man East of the Missouri. And everyone came and sat together.

"You must drink your milk, Mademoiselle Olivia," said the Famous Zorofsky. "Otherwise you will have no strength to walk the big wire one day!" Olivia could only walk a small wire in her clown shoes.

"And don't forget your peas, *ma petite*," warned Monsieur Jeanette. "They make you clever and wise, *non*? Already you know not to juggle in front of my elephants."

Everyone nodded. Including the Great Funnybones. Like most circus people, he was very superstitious.

Next morning, the Crystal Caravan had visitors. The sound of elephants trumpeting and tigers roaring drew the folks of Homersville like lodestone.

"I have an empty field," offered a farmer named Thorstaad. "Your animals are welcome to graze there while you're here."

So later, it was Olivia, of course, who was sent to tend them.

At the Thorstaad farm, she was met by a woman in an old slat bonnet and overalls.

"Morning," she said. "I'm Mrs. Thorstaad. You must be Olivia." She led the way to a field where black-and-white cows shared clover with the elephants. And while Olivia brushed Bull's Eye's mane and braided Azarah's tail, Mrs. Thorstaad kept her company.

When Monsieur Jeanette came to get the animals for the four o'clock show, Olivia hated to leave.

"Why not let the child sit a spell?" urged Mrs. Thorstaad. "I'll see that she gets back in time."

Olivia held her breath. When Monsieur Jeanette said "*Oui*," her heart leaped. Higher even than the Famous Zorofsky.

No one paid much attention to the big clouds that had begun moving in from the west.

Olivia and Mrs. Thorstaad made their way back through the field to the farmhouse. As they did, Olivia heard the sound of a school bell.

Clang, clang, clang! it called to her.

How Olivia'd always dreamed of going to school too! But a real school. At the Crystal Caravan, the only teacher she'd ever had was the Great Funnybones. He taught her from books that were old and worn, and Olivia kept these under her bed, next to her clown shoes.

When she wished for a real school and real learning, her father would say, "You're a clown child. You have sawdust in your blood. You know things most folks never will."

In the farmhouse, Olivia didn't know where to look first. Shiny floorboards squeaked when she walked. A rocking chair met her in the parlor. She saw curtains at the windows, and wallpaper on the walls—just as she'd imagined.

But off in the kitchen, she saw the best thing of all. A bathtub on fancy little feet. At the Crystal Caravan, Olivia was lucky to get a bucket of water to wash in each night.

After Mrs. Thorstaad made them some tea and krumkakes, Olivia continued to stare at the tub.

"Child," Mrs. Thorstaad asked her kindly, "would you like to take a bath?"

Would she! As Olivia watched, Mrs. Thorstaad took a monstrous kettle from the stove and filled the tub with steaming water. She handed Olivia a towel and a bar of soap. The minute Mrs. Thorstaad left the room, Olivia unfastened her overalls and climbed right in. Something smelled like roses.

"I'm in a house," marveled Olivia, and she soaked in that tub for the longest time, never noticing the room had grown lavender blue. Then black as pitch.

The rain startled her first. It nailed against the house. But it was the wind screaming across the prairie that made her jump to her feet. Olivia shivered. This was no ordinary storm.

Might be a blowdown, she thought. All circus people knew about blowdowns. Those fast-moving storms that could snatch tent tops and poles in nothing flat.

At the Crystal Caravan, everyone saw the storm too. The show had already begun when lightning licked the tent top. Now the Famous Zorofsky thought twice about walking the steel wire, and Monsieur Jeanette's tigers refused to perform.

The ringmaster had to make a decision. Stay, or shut down the circus and move to higher ground. Maybe to the next town. The Great Funnybones said nothing. He was thinking about Olivia.

"She's safe right where she is," said the ringmaster to him. And he ordered everyone to leave the tent.

By nightfall it was raining even harder. At the Thorstaad farm, Mr. Thorstaad came into the kitchen soaking wet.

"River's rising," he said grimly.

Mrs. Thorstaad held Olivia close. "Don't fret, honey," she said. "Your pa'll come soon as he can."

Olivia nodded bravely. But inside she felt like she was facing Monsieur Jeanette's tigers.

Later, Mrs. Thorstaad read her a story and put her to sleep in a soft feather bed. Olivia wished she could enjoy it. The rain flung itself on the world in a great tantrum, and she dreamed that her clown shoes floated downriver.

For the next three days it rained and rained. The river swelled, then flooded, and the road washed out—clear to the town of Lonetree. Poor Olivia. Each morning she stood at the parlor window, looking out. Hoping to see a wagon. But none came.

Finally, one morning Mrs. Thorstaad announced, "I'm going to show you how to make krumkakes." And she did.

The next day, Mrs. Thorstaad taught Olivia a tune on the upright in the parlor. Olivia nearly forgot to be sad. And they both taught her how to play checkers in the evenings after supper. Olivia always won.

And then one morning, the sun reappeared.

"Road's still out, though," said Mr. Thorstaad. "It looks like it might be out at least for another week."

Mrs. Thorstaad looked excited. "School starts next week. Perhaps you'd like to go, child."

Olivia did. At first. But would that mean she might stay here forever? She looked out the window again, past the wild plum, down the road toward the town of Lonetree.

Then, the next afternoon, Mrs. Thorstaad's quilting party came to call. No rising river was going to stop them. Once a month they all met to socialize over their latest quilt pattern. Today it was "Kansas Troubles." But even more troubling to the ladies was the sight of Olivia pouring tea in the kitchen.

"Martha Thorstaad," demanded one. "Have you taken leave of your senses? A clown child! In your own home!"

"Hush, Jenny," scolded Mrs. Thorstaad. "She'll hear you."

"I don't care. Circus people aren't like real folks."

"Nonsense," said Mrs. Thorstaad. "Olivia's real all right. She even wants to go to school."

School! Mrs. Thorstaad's quilting party was horrified. The plain fact was, circus children didn't go to school.

"Martha," said Jenny firmly, "everyone knows circus children ain't much on learnin'!"

Olivia couldn't believe her ears. At first she felt like crying—until she remembered. She was a clown child. She had sawdust in her blood. She knew things Mrs. Thorstaad's quilting party never would. She had to set them straight.

Olivia marched into the room and stood before them.

"Ladies!" she said in her best ringmaster's voice. "How many of your children know never to stand in front of an elephant?"

Skirts rustled. A thimble dropped.

"Can any of them do this?" Olivia snatched up several pincushions, balancing them all on the tip of her nose.

"Or this?" And she grabbed up three napkins and made them disappear. The quilting party was speechless.

"And can they walk a wire," asked the Amazing Pickles, "only six inches from the ground?" Pretending to wear her big clown shoes, Olivia showed them how, weaving and wobbling across a crack in the floor. It was the funniest part of her act.

But she tripped on a stool. Martha laughed.

"Clown children love to be laughed at!" Olivia said. And for a moment she stood there, head held high. Then, she took a sweeping bow and left the room.

Olivia ran to the barn. There she could cry all to herself.

"Pa," she asked out loud, "where are you?"

Right then, Olivia thought of something. Something she loved and had almost forgotten.

One, two, three, four. She picked up four eggs and juggled. In a steady rhythm she sent them sailing into the air.

The hen clucked. The pig squealed. The cow lowed. Olivia's heart soared. And suddenly she heard a familiar voice.

"That's my girl!"

One, two, three—four. A hand reached out and caught the last egg.

"Pa," she cried, throwing herself in his arms and holding on tight. "Pa, you've come!"

That night, Mrs. Thorstaad made a special dinner in honor of Olivia and the Great Funnybones. Soon, though, it was time to go.

"I'm gonna miss you, honey," Mrs. Thorstaad said, holding Olivia close.

Olivia missed her already. And the wild plum tree growing outside her window, and going to school.

But not nearly as much as never sitting down to supper with the Famous Zorofsky, Monsieur Jeanette, or the Tallest Man East of the Missouri. Not as much as never seeing the Crystal Caravan again.

"I'll see you next summer," she promised, waving good-bye.

The wagon moved on, yet it hadn't gone far when the Great Funnybones yelled, "Whoa!"

"Look, Pickles." He smiled. "Yonder. In that yellow field. Three white horses all in a row!"

Olivia nodded. "Good luck for sure, Pa," she said. For she felt lucky too—lucky and glad that Bull's Eye was taking them to the next circus town.